David Tetlow was born in Rossendale, Lancashire during the Second World War. Following his school years, he worked as a mechanical engineer and later specialised in textile machinery research and development. He married Joyce in 1963 and has a son, daughter, four grandchildren and recently two great-grandchildren. He joined the Lancashire police in the late 1960s and completed most of his thirty years-service in the Greater Manchester police from which he retired as an investigating officer.

I have written this book in dedication to the father of a good friend, Jan Dolecki. Whenever I met Jan, he always had a welcoming warm and friendly smile on his face. He died quite recently well and into his nineties. Born in Poland, Jan was taken prisoner as a teenager in World War II by the invading Russian army, and suffered all and more of the indignities mentioned in this part-fact, part-fictional book. He was sent to Siberia, was later released, then joined the Polish army and fought at Monte Cassino.

# David Tetlow

# THE AGONY OF POLAND

Best Wishes

AUSTIN MACAULEY PUBLISHERS™

LONDON · CAMBRIDGE · NEW YORK · SHARJAH

A CIP catalogue record for this title is available from the British Library.

ISBN 9781035821273 (Paperback)
ISBN 9781035821280 (ePub e-book)

www.austinmacauley.com

First Published 2024
Austin Macauley Publishers Ltd®
1 Canada Square
Canary Wharf
London
E14 5AA

To Jan Dolecki's family for their assistance and allowing me to write this book.

# Prologue

In the latter part of 1939, the German leader Adolph Hitler, decided to invade Poland. He must have been aware that this was a gamble. The Wehrmacht (German army) was not quite yet at full strength and his generals urged caution. Hitler however, was confident that an invasion of Poland would be short and sharp. He was also convinced that the British and French leaders, Chamberlain and Daladier, would opt for a peace settlement rather than declare war. Hitler's certainty was obviously based on the fact that during the past few years, Britain and France had accepted various moves, including the full rearmament of the German army. Hitler's main concern at the time, appeared to the reaction of the Soviet Union to such an invasion. The result was that following a meeting between Hitler and Stalin, they came to an agreement, (The Von Ribbentrop-Molotov Pact), to restore the pre-1919 borders. The German army would invade from the north, south and west, and without a formal declaration of war, the Soviet's would invade from the east.

On the 1st of September 1939, Germany invaded Poland. Britain immediately declared war.

On the 17th of September, the Soviet army invaded from the east.

# Chapter One

It was August 1939, and the Polish family Jakub and Adriana Gorka, a couple in their early forties, farmed in the beautiful Polish countryside ten kilometres east of the town of Belz. It was a comparatively small dairy farm of twenty acres. Jakub's mother had died some years before and his father Dariusz was now too ill and bedridden to assist with the day to day running of the farm.

Dariusz had been given the land in 1920 by the newly appointed Polish Government as a reward for his heroic conduct during a war in the 1918-1920 period, land which was disputed and claimed by the Soviet Union. The farmhouse and barn were simple wooden structures built by Jakub's father twenty years before. Water was gained from a stream which ran close to the house. Heating and cooking was also a simple matter, using a coal stove on a stone platform inside the kitchen. They had no electricity. Lighting came from several oil lanterns, and the toilets were outside pits situated in a wooden shelter, which were moved when the need arose.

The land they controlled was large enough to contain forty head of milk cows, a good bull, which was often sent to other neighbouring farmers, who reciprocated to avoid any cross contamination. They also ran beef cattle, and made butter and cheese for their own and local consumption, and for the Belz market.

They had a son and daughter, Filip and Alicja. Filip, a strong, sturdy youth, was 17, and Alicja, a very beautiful, young woman, was 18. They had now finished their schooling at the age of sixteen, and the four were a happy family running a successful small business, making their living by selling their produce at the Friday market in Belz.

It was Friday 25$^{th}$ of August. Filip and Alicja had been given the job, which they loved, of travelling into the town each week, taking the pony and cart with the week's saleable beef, milk, cheese and butter produce, where they would normally spend most of the day running their regular market stall. Alicja was particularly fond of the task because it was the only time she could meet up with the man she had fallen in love with, 20-year-old Boris Batrosz, the son of a vegetable farmer, who lived several kilometres to the west of the town, who also stood in the market every Friday.

Boris lived with his father and mother on the farm where they produced many crops, again mainly for sale at the Belz market.

Travelling the route they knew so well in the dark, they arrived at six o'clock, then set up their stall as usual among other market people. As they did so, they became aware that something different was in the air. The stallholders were speaking to each other in low voices and seemed subdued.

It was becoming daylight when Alicja approached the nearby stallholder, the love of her life, Boris, and they kissed.

'Boris, there is something going on. What is it?'

'Nothing to worry about. It's just a rumour in town that the Germans may be about to invade Poland. I don't know where it started but I am sure it's just rubbish. In any case we have a strong Polish army – they would not dare.'

The day continued to be different in that they had sold all their produce and were able to pack up to leave by the late morning. Alicja again approached Boris.

'I don't understand it. We are normally here all day. We have sold out and the whole market is packing to go.'

Boris replied. 'I can only think that people are panic buying because of the rumours. Ah well, we get an early finish.'

Because it was so early in the day, the pair decided to take some time off and to wander through the town holding hands, with poor Filip playing gooseberry. The town was rife with gossip, many people clearly believing that the Germans were about to invade and that Poland would soon be at war. Boris however was optimistic, stating that even if they did invade, they would be repulsed by the strong Polish army and would never reach Belz.

Walking by the River Solokiya, he asked Filip to stay seated on the grass while he walked along the river bank with Alicja. When they were out of sight, he quickly went down on one knee, looked Alicja in the eyes, produced a ring and said simply, 'Will you marry me?'

With tears in her eyes she said, 'I thought that you would never ask. Yes, yes, yes. But you will have to get permission from my father.'

Putting the ring back in his pocket, he said, 'I will take time off on Sunday and will ride out to see your father, then the ring is yours.'

She laughed and said, 'If he agrees'.

Two days later, Boris set off at first light from his father's farm, riding one of the obliging farm horses to travel the seventeen kilometres through the good fertile land, to visit and appeal for the hand of Alicja in marriage.

On arrival, he was made most welcome by the family, who were well aware of the reason for the visit. The whole family including Dariusz were determined, in a kind and humorous way, to sweat him a little and make him as nervous as possible. Adriana had made a sumptuous meal and home-made wine was available.

At the conclusion of the meal, the family, as previously planned, sat around the table with simple smiles on their faces. No one spoke, and they all looked at Boris expectantly.

Eventually Boris said, 'Jakub, can I speak to you alone?'

Jakub frowned teasingly and said, 'No, anything you say can be said in front of us all for consideration.'

Boris, who by now, sweating and feeling very uncomfortable, swallowed and quickly said, 'Alicja and I would like to marry and am here for your consent and blessing.'

At that, the whole family and eventually, when the penny dropped, Boris, burst out in fits of laughter.

'Welcome to our family,' said Jakub, pouring large glasses of wine for everyone.

Boris made a great play of, again, going down on one knee and handing the ring to Alicja.

They spent the afternoon in good spirits until it became time for the late afternoon milking. Boris set off home to arrive before dark. Alicja saw him go with a big smile on her face. This was the last time she would see him for several years.

# Chapter Two

Five days later, on the 1st September, and in accordance with the MolotovRibbentrop Pact, Germany invaded Poland from the north, south and west, an action which became known as the Blitzkrieg of Poland.

Contrary to the beliefs of Boris and many other Polish people at the time, the Blitzkrieg was very successful as much a result of Polish vulnerability as it was to do with German superiority.

Poland is chiefly flat land and at that time, the ground was hard, which was ideal for rapid advance.

The Germans possessed overwhelming equipment and numbers, and they were aware that the Soviets would very soon attack from the east.

Air pilot Albin Andrysiak knew the massive strength and superior quality of the Luftwaffe and had spent, what may be his last night on earth, at the Warsaw airbase with his wife Olga, a Polish Airforce nurse.

That morning, after a tearful farewell, he and 175 of his comrades took off in their PZL P11 fighter aircraft from the Air Force base just outside the city to engage the enemy. Even though they were vastly outnumbered and facing much more modern aircraft, and they lost many men and aircraft during the clash, they succeeded in bringing down 170 enemy aircraft before the situation became untenable, their airport destroyed and what was left of the Polish Air Force had to break off the fight before their fuel ran out and head for the relative safety of the Mions airfield in France.

Albin, like many of his colleagues, was devastated that he had been forced to leave his wife behind in Warsaw. He prayed that one day they would be reunited. He, and others, were forced to put those feelings aside and maintain an excellent moral and relish the opportunity to one day re-engage the enemy.

The Polish Air Force (Polskie Sily Powietrzne) was destined to fight in the battle of France as one Fighter Squadron GC1/145 Warsaw. Sixteen flights of Polish pilots and ground crew were detached to French Fighter Squadrons and later took part in the combat. This core of the Polish Air Units were veterans of the 1939 invasion.

Albins opportunity came in May 1940 when the German army invaded France, and again, the Polish Air Force excelled themselves in a vastly uneven contest, by bringing down many German aircraft before having, again, to relocate this time to East Church in Kent, where they became part of the British Air Force.

The Royal Air Force welcomed into its ranks thousands of exiles from German occupied Poland. Polish personnel served in all commands and earned a reputation for exceptional courage and devotion to duty.

In the meanwhile, his wife Olga, who was equally devastated at losing her husband, not knowing whether or not he had survived the German onslaught, was captured by the German army in her Warsaw hospital and forced, with threats to her remaining family, to use her nursing talents in German Field Hospitals on their behalf.

Belz, and all the countryside around there, were on the west side of the River Solokyia and the area, which was heavily populated by Jewish people, was quickly taken by Germany.

The Gorka family, who lived just a few kilometres away from the town, were well aware of the invasion, and besides grieving for the township, they wondered when the Germans would take over their farm and what would happen to them. Alicja wanted to go to find her Boris and bring him to the farm, but was not allowed to do so by her father.

'I have heard that there is a curfew. They do not allow anyone out on the streets or countryside. Anyone caught is simply shot.'

They were, of course, unaware of the pact between the Soviet Union and Germany. On the 17th September, Russia invaded from the east. There was little resistance. It took only sixteen days for them to occupy the whole of eastern Poland.

Time went on and the Gorka family began to think that they were to be left alone and able to carry on with their farming activities.

The morning of the 6th October 1939, they saw an army truck arrive at the farm, and six soldiers alight from it carrying rifles with attached bayonets. The family fearfully realised how wrong they had been. The soldiers quickly gathered the family together outside the front of the house, threatening them with their rifles. They, at first, assumed that they were German, until one spoke in the language of Russia which they could partially understand.

'You are Polish occupiers of the land of the Soviet Union which you stole from us many years ago. Therefore you are enemies of the Soviet Union and prisoners of war. You will be taken from here and this farm will be returned to a Soviet family.'

Dariusz, who was in his bed, could hear a commotion outside, went to the window and could hear what was said. He was incensed.

'They are not taking my land from my family,' he growled to himself.

The soldier barked, 'You may take clothing, food, and drink with you. We will leave here soon.'

Jakub said, 'You can't do that. What about my father? He is bedridden.'

As he said it, Dariusz stumbled through the door carrying the scatter gun he had used to keep the wolves from his animal. He did not point the gun at anyone and he shouted, 'Get off my land.'

The six soldiers raised their rifles as one and fired. Dariusz chest and shoulders were ripped apart and he flew through the air as if he had been hit by a train, stone dead as he landed on the ground. Adriana and Alicja screamed in mental agony and began to run towards the body when they were blocked by the soldiers.

'Put them in the truck and one of you stay with them,' shouted the Russian.

They were hysterical as they were forced into the truck. The rear doors remained open and the guard sat at the rear quietly muttering something the family could not quite understand.

'If you move he will kill you,' shouted their Soviet leader.

The heartbroken, grieving family could see, from the situation, the body of their father, father-in-law and grandfather lying on the ground. Jakub shouted, 'We need to give him a Christian burial.'

They were totally ignored by the soldiers. They saw two of the soldiers carry the body across the farmyard and out of their sight. The two Russians carried the body to the cattle dung heap and threw him on top. He sank out of sight.

Four other army trucks rolled up into the farmyard and a short time later, the family could hear shooting. They were hopeful that the Polish army had caught up with the Soviets. Their hopes were shattered when the Russian approached completely unperturbed.

'What was the shooting?' asked Jakub.

'A large army need plenty of food. You have plenty which you now don't need. The trucks you see are our butchers. We have cleared the farm of animals and their dairy milk, cheese and butter. We will soon be ready to leave.'

'We need to bury our father.'

'He has already been buried,' he replied with a smirk on his face.

'You promised us food, and we need clothing take with us.'

'The promise was made before your family attacked us. You will leave as you are. If you argue more, we will take you naked.'

One of the Soviet soldiers approached and said in Russian, which the family again could largely understand, 'They need to take warm clothing and food. We need work from them, otherwise, when we get to the railway station, we will be forced to clothe and feed them, and you will not be popular.'

'Okay,' he said. 'You will be escorted into the house, and you may get your warmest clothing. You will need it where you are going. Take whatever food you can find. Hurry, we will leave very soon.'

Jakub nodded his thanks to the Soviet, who grunted in return. They were allowed to return to the house where they packed what they could into hessian sacks.

Back in the truck, they faced an uncomfortable journey which seemed to take several hours. Their leader had taken a seat in the front of the truck, and their guards would not, or could not explain what was to happen. Eventually, the truck stopped, and they were ordered out. What they then saw was utter confusion. Hundreds of fellow Polish people on a Railway Station platform, some crying, others with dour stoic faces, being guarded by many Soviet soldiers. Jakub looked around to see where they were and saw the sign Lubomyrka railway station.

He approached a man of similar age to himself and asked, 'Do you know why we are here?'

To their horror he replied, 'We are all regarded as prisoners of war and we are being transported to Siberia in the Soviet Union as slave labour.'

They were forced to wait for several hours, eventually finding a space where they could sit on the cold stone ground, as more and more miserable Polish people were herded into the railway compound until, at last, the train arrived.

# Chapter Three

On the 27<sup>th</sup> September, ten days before the Gorka family were transported, Boris's father Kamil and mother Agata were working on their farm when they began to hear explosions and gunfire in the distance, coming nearer by the hour. Boris was with them, and they decided to hide from the conflict in the farmhouse, which was a solid, stone-built house where they hoped that they would be safe. Through the window, Boris saw Polish soldiers retreating towards them with German Panzer tanks shelling them from the distance and Nazi aircraft machine gunning them. The Germans were clearly heading towards the town of Belz. Some of the Polish soldiers ran into the farmyard taking shelter behind the stone walls.

The tank commanders obviously saw them and directed their fire at the walls. Boris saw that one very young Polish soldier had been hit by shrapnel and was writhing in agony in the farmyard. He set off to assist the soldier. His mother shouted at him not to go as it was too dangerous. He went anyway and saved his life.

A German bomber passed overhead, releasing a bomb which directly hit the farmhouse, the explosion killing everyone inside.

The young soldier died in his arms. Boris was in a state of shock. Everything had happened so quickly. Sobbing, he ran towards the grain store remembering something he had done as a boy many times before as a prank, hiding from his parents. He pulled his jacket over his head and face, allowing himself to sink into a large vat of Barley until it covered him completely. He was not in too deep and could breathe easily.

Trying to control his sobbing, he could hear that the shooting and bombing had stopped. Then he heard loud German voices close by. They were obviously looking for Polish soldiers. He heard Polish voices calling for a retreat. The shooting began again nearby, then it went quiet.

He remained where he was for another hour before emerging into a hell zone. The house in which he had grown up had been reduced to rubble. He was devastated and shouting, hoping that his parents had survived even though his heart told him that it was not possible. He could see five dead Polish soldiers around the ruined farmhouse.

During the following six days, Boris could hear gunfire and explosions in the distance. The fighting was still going on and no one approached the farm. Boris pulled away rubble until he found his almost unrecognisable dead father and mother. He created a graveyard by digging a deep and wide pit, giving his parents and the soldiers a respectful Christian burial. All the time he was employed with this debilitating and gruesome task, he could still hear shooting and explosions coming from the direction of Belz. The ever-faithful horse had survived the attack on the farm. On the morning of the tenth day, the war noises coming from Belz had ceased. Boris said his final prayers over the grave, took whatever food and money he could find, saddled the horse and thinking of Alicja, he rode away with the intention of never returning.

Boris knew the area well, and stayed in the wooded hill areas close to the road north of Belz, heading towards the Gorka dairy farm. As he drew close to Belz, he saw a huge silent crowd of people on foot, carrying luggage in various forms and clearly guarded by German soldiers, some in vehicles and some on foot. He hid behind trees and watched, wondering what was happening. As they passed below him, he recognised many of the people passing. Some were friends and fellow market stall holders, others had been customers for several years. All were Jews. Boris had no idea what was happening, and he hoped that they were being peacefully taken to live elsewhere. He could not in his wildest dreams have imagined the truth.

He rode on, keeping to the deep countryside, until with deep shock, he arrived at the Gorka farm. Carcasses of dead cattle were scattered in the fields, farmyard and barn. There were just heads, hides and bones left. They had been crudely butchered. The smell of rotting flesh was unbearable.

As he walked past the dung heap, he saw to his horror, what appeared to be the shape of a human foot covered in filth, protruding from the edge of the heap. His first dreadful thoughts were 'Could this be Alicia murdered by the Soviets.' In great trepidation and without any thought for himself, he seized the ankle and pulled the body covered in filth from the mire. Still unable to identify it, he picked up an empty milk churn, ran to the nearby stream, he filled the churn with water, ran back to the body and poured water over the head and shoulders, and to his later shame, he was relieved to see the contorted and wizened face of Dariusz.

Boris again performed the heart-breaking task of giving another well respected person a Christian burial, constantly apologising for his feeling of relief when he first viewed the dead face.

He searched the farmhouse to find that the family had clearly left in a hurry and the place had been ransacked. Boris was desolate. He had lost his father, mother and the farm in which he had hoped would be his future, and now he had lost his sweetheart, the girl he wanted to spend the rest of his life with. He sat in the wrecked kitchen feeling desolate and thinking. 'What could he do now? How could he help to restore his country back to the control of the Polish People? Where was Alicja? Was she still alive?' He did not know. 'How can I find out?' he thought.

He was aware that a family named Adamik lived on a smallholding just a kilometre away, and perhaps they had the information he was seeking. Boris set off on horseback to find out. As he approached the smallholding, he saw from a distance that there was smoke coming from the chimney. He approached warily and dismounted just a short distance from the gateway, when a man wearing a Soviet soldier's uniform. and carrying a rifle, walked out of the front door, pointing the rifle at Boris. He shouted in Russian, which Boris understood. 'Come towards me.'

He leapt back on his horse, slapping its rump, digging in his heels and shouting. The horse understood and took off as quickly as it could, back the way they had travelled. Boris heard shots and a wild whistling, whirring noise as a bullet passed close to his head.

Back at the farm, Boris was now very much aware that he had to leave Poland if he was to be of any help in restoring the country. But where? If he travelled east, there was only the massive Soviet Union. South, he was aware lay Czechoslovakia, Hungary and Austria. North, the Baltic countries and the sea. He had to travel west, hoping to get to Denmark, France, or the Netherlands, but that would take him through Germany, he was completely at a loss.

He searched for food and found a large piece of cheese which had been missed by the invaders. He also found a pack of canvas in which he could wrap up against the night's cold, and he set off west on horseback, without any real plan. As he approached Belz, he was in a wooded area when he heard shooting. He dismounted, tethering the horse and hiding among the trees. He could see below, that a group of Polish soldiers who had probably been in hiding and were attempting to escape from the Belz area, had run into a smaller group of Soviet soldiers. It was just beginning to go dark, and the Poles were clearly winning the fight. He heard the Soviets shouting to each. He saw at least two Soviets fall.

As it became dark, the shooting ceased, and from what he could hear, the Poles had made their escape. Boris crept from his position to where he had seen a soldier fall. He felt and shook the shoulder of the soldier who did not move. He tried the soldier's trouser pockets. They were empty. He moved his hand to the tunic pocket, unbuttoned it and could feel two cards inside. As he took the cards, he saw in the distance a lantern had been lit and heard Russian voices approaching and shouting for their comrades. Boris quickly and silently made his way back to the trees. Hoping that he would not be discovered, he wrapped himself in canvas near his horse and fell asleep. He woke at first light and going back to the edge of the trees, he looked down and could see no evidence of the previous evening's brief fierce battle. He opened and examined the two cards, and found that he had the identity cards, one red and the other brown, of a Russian soldier named Olek Adamovich. He gazed at the soldier's photograph in the red card, and realised that the young, unshaven face could be mistaken for him. Could this be his passport to Western Europe? That morning, his mind made up, Boris began his perilous long journey across German held Poland, towards the German border.

# Chapter Four

At Lubomyrka railway station, after a long, cold wait, Jakub, Adriana, Alicja, and Filip were unceremoniously pushed into the cargo carriage of a train with hundreds of others. There was so much pushing and confusion, that they had to hold hands to make certain that the entered the same carriage.

Seventy people were pushed into one carriage which had no seats and had not been designed for passengers. The Gorka family were among the first on board, and found a small corner with two wide shelves where they could be together and defend the food and clothing they had been allowed to bring. There were no beds, blankets, or any other kind of creature comfort to be had, and it soon became clear that any food they needed during the journey, was that which they had brought with them.

Once everyone was aboard, the train set off on what was to become a slow, week-long journey, into the cold winter of the freezing northern Siberia.

Most of the passengers were families like the Gorkas, with warm clothing and provisions. There were two babies and several young children. Four young men and three young women appeared to be alone. They were not warmly dressed and did not appear to be carrying any food.

Three armed Russian guards walked into the carriage, pushing people to each side, and gesturing along the centre of the carriage, clearly indicating that a path should be left unobstructed for their access.

'How long will we be on this train?' asked one of the young mothers. One of the guards who clearly understood the question shrugged and muttered in Russian something that sounded like 'Long time'.

Adriana asked, 'Where are the toilets?'

The same guard smiled and pointed to the corner of the carriage to a hole in the floor, where the railway line and sleepers could be seen rushing by underneath. He pushed his way to a shelf and pulled out a rough bench, which had a hole cut into the middle of it. He placed the bench over the hole and said, 'Toilet.'

'What about food?' someone said.

'How do we wash?' another asked.

The guards shrugged and walked onto the next carriage without another word.

A middle-aged man, who, during the journey, became a good friend of Jakub, Bartek Bosko, stood and asked for attention.

'We have to make this journey. We have no choice. So let us try to survive by looking after each other as best we can. We are travelling into the cold climate of Siberia which most of us have never felt before. I see that some of the young people have no warm clothing. I have a little spare so I will give a warm coat to one of the young men. If we are not given food, we have to share what we have. Do you agree?'

Most of the company nodded and signalled their agreement, and the makings of a small, very uncomfortable community was born.

Some clothing was shared, and the young people expressed their gratitude. The young men pulled two high shelves down and arranged them so that people using the toilet had a degree of privacy.

People slept that first night as best they could on shelves or on the floor. The following morning, their first on the train, people were hoping that food and water of some kind would be provided. Nothing came.

They all had with them food of sorts, some of it very meagre. Bartek and Jakub warned people to ration their supplies.

It began to snow heavily, and later that day, the train stopped at a station to take on water and coal. It took the passengers a while to realise that this was an opportunity to become hydrated by sucking the snow and melting it in their mouths.

The guards had no worries about prisoners escaping. It was clearly apparent that they had nowhere to escape to, and those who tried would die of cold and starvation.

Without any warning, the train set off, and prisoners who were still outside had to run quickly to get aboard. A middle-aged woman, who had clearly gone behind some nearby trees to get some toiletry privacy, began to limp a quickly as she could in an impossible task to re-join the train. The passengers in the last carriage could hear the Russian soldiers at the rear laughing and shouting, 'Target practice.' They heard shooting and one man, who could see what was happening through a knot hole in the rear of the carriage, expressed the opinion that he was glad for her sake that they had put her out of her misery.

Even though the train was their only lifeline, after a few days, people began to die of lack of any nourishment and extreme cold. The many babies on the train were the worst hit, because the mal-nourished mothers could not provide the milk. Their poor bodies were simply and contemptuously discarded by the guards. At each stop during the final days of travel, adult and children's bodies were unceremoniously dumped from the train.

After one week to the day, the train arrived with the survivors at Czelabinkaja railway station for transport to the Czepasewka Posiolek labour camp. More commonly known as a Gulag.

# Chapter Five

Boris was travelling by horse across the 650 kilometres stretch of Western Poland towards the German border, which, unknown to him at that time, was not heavily manned, the Germans having claimed the whole of western Poland as their own. He was keeping to the forests, hills, and countryside. As a country man from his early days, he was well aware of what he could pick to eat for himself and the horse, and he occasionally stopped at farms still operated by Polish farmers who were being forced to feed the German army, offering a few days labour for money and food.

His journey was going, very well. After several days, he had reached a spot to the north of Poznan, and the only German troops he had encountered were foot soldiers that were easy to avoid by riding quickly away.

He was riding through a forest area, when he suddenly heard German voices shouting very loudly. He stopped dead in his tracks and tethered the horse to a tree, moving forward slowly, looking from a hilltop into a small valley below. What he saw during the next few moments would stay with him for the rest of his life. A dozen German guards were standing before an equal number of Polish soldiers who appeared to be of higher rank, and were digging in the stony soil into which they were shoulder deep. Boris assumed, in his naivety, that they were digging for a good reason, but he could not understand what. He shrugged and decided to circle well around this area. He was about to leave, when the Germans suddenly opened fire, killing all within the pit. Boris was stunned. He lay there, unable to believe what he had just seen and too frightened to move. He watched the soldiers bring forward a tractor with a large blade on the front and push the soil back into the pit, running backwards and forwards over it until the ground was flat and even. The soldiers eventually moved away, and Boris stood with tears streaming down his cheeks and stumbled back to his horse.

Until his experiences of the last few weeks, he had lived a hard-working, loving life, not aware of the world's evils. His attitudes were quickly hardening, and he was becoming more and more determined to reach western Europe and play some part in evening up the score.

Boris was still a civilian, entirely alone, completely unaware that Polish soldiers were escaping in large numbers to fight again. They were travelling to Split in Yugoslavia, or to the Baltic States, then by sea to Malta and France, and that the Polish air force was relocating to France and Britain. He was heading towards the old German border.

He travelled on westwards, avoiding towns and villages, until late one afternoon, he came to the area of Zelon Gola which he believed to be close to the German border. He found a dairy farm which he watched for a while, until he was certain that the workers were Polish and likely to have some sympathy for him and his situation.

It was, by now, early December 1939. Boris approached the farm on seeing an elderly man walking from the farmhouse

31

towards the fields. The man viewed him suspiciously as he rode towards him.

'Who are you and what do you want?' he said with narrowed eyes.

'I am Boris and I am looking for work,' he replied.

'Where are you from?'

'I am from a farm near Belz. I am a farm worker. My horse is a bit thin and tired at the moment. He needs feeding and a rest, but he is a good farm horse.'

The old man began to warm towards Boris.

'You also look a bit thin and tired. I have heard that Belz was completely destroyed by the Germans. Why are you here?'

Boris felt compelled to tell the truth, no matter how the old man might take it.

'The Germans killed my parents and I think that the Russians have stolen from me the love of my life. I am intending to reach France and take up arms against them, but first I need to work and earn a little money to help with my journey.'

'Then you have to understand that the reason we are still open for business is that we are being forced to help to feed the German army. I have need for a good horse and a good worker. In conscience, can you work for me?'

'Needs must, I fear. For one month. Yes.'

The pair shook hands, and the farmer, Jan Chlebek, took the horse to the stables where he was fed, and Boris to the farmhouse, and for the next four weeks a new friendship grew.

Over the first hot meal Boris had eaten in days, Jan opened his heart to him, telling him that months before, when war with Germany was looming, his son Alek had left home joining the Polish army. He had not seen him since, and was afraid he may never see him again.

After the meal, it was mid-evening and dark. Jan took Boris to a small bedroom and said, 'This is my son's room. You may sleep here during your stay. I want you up early in the morning for milking. You may as well go to bed now.'

Boris was very tired and grateful. He had sheets and blankets and warmth after many cold nights. After Jan left him alone, he stripped, lay on the bed, and was asleep within seconds.

He was roused by Jan well before light the next morning, to find clean water in a bowl and warm clothing at the foot of the bed. He washed and dressed. In the kitchen he found Jan with fresh baked bread and cheese, and a hot drink.

'You say that you are a farmer,' said Jan, 'so you will be skilled at milking cattle.'

'No, sorry, we were crop farmers – wheat, barley, and maze. I have never milked a cow, but I am ready and willing to learn.'

Jan smiled.

'It will take at least ten minutes to teach you.'

Over the next few days, Jan and Boris got to know each other well. Jan had lost his wife years before and had run the farm together with his only son. Jan was now alone, employing workers from a nearby village, one of whom, Gust, was the farm manager among his many other duties.

Boris, who was used to hard work, soon settled into the various jobs required of him on a dairy farm. Milking the cattle twice a day was only the beginning he found. Between the milking, he became engaged in feeding the bullocks, taking the cows and heifers to the bull, and the long and laborious stirring of the milk in the butter and cheese making shed.

Working at least twelve hours a day, seven days a week would discourage most young men, but Boris was now at his happiest since the loss of his parents and Alicia.

At the end of Boris's first week, Jan spoke to him over the evening meal.

'Boris, I would be very pleased if you would change your mind about travelling west to fight. I have grown very fond of you. Please stay here and help me to run this farm.'

'Jan, I feel the same. You have become a second father to me. I am sorry, but I must continue my journey before I get too comfortable here.'

'How do you mean to travel?'

'I have the cards of a Russian soldier who was killed a few weeks back.'

He showed the identification cards to Jan.

'I intend to travel by train through Germany as an ally of their army, a wounded Russian soldier, to reach a family, which I will invent, living in the far west of Germany using these cards.'

'Do you speak Russian?'

'Our language is very similar.'

'Do you speak German?'

'No, and that may be a serious problem.'

'If you will not stay here, I will help you as much as I can.'

'Gust was born and raised near the German border. He speaks fluent German. He has also lost sons to the Polish army. I am sure he will teach you. I receive payment for some of my goods in Reichsmarks. I will pay you for your services and buy your horse before you leave.'

During the following three weeks, Boris rose early and worked on the farm until mid-afternoon when he would sit for at least an hour with Gust, who was very supportive of his intentions to learn, as best he could, the rudiments of the German language, which was not any way similar to Polish. In this way, he prepared himself for the most dangerous part of his journey.

# Chapter Six

Jakub, Adriana, Alicja, and Filip, and around seven hundred others, were ordered from the relative warmth of the train into temperatures of -20 degrees, and forced into open trucks for transportation to Czepasewka Posiolek Gulag.

On seeing them shivering and gasping for breath into cold air, the guards laughed and shouted in Russian which they could mainly understand.

'You will get used to it or die.'

At the Gulag, the large group were forced to stand in the cold and await the head of the camp for instructions and warnings. When they came, it was a simple message.

'Get used to the cold, work hard, or you will not eat and you will die.'

They were instructed to attend a parade at 7am sharp the next morning, when they would be allocated with their employment. The family were then ushered into a two-roomed, small wooden hut, which was to be their future home. At least they were pleased with the privacy. There were two hard wooden beds and blankets in the hut. When the family examined them, they were found to be crawling with bedbugs and lice. They took them outside and beat and shook them to be rid of the incursion as best they could. A stove was situated in one of the rooms, without any signs of fuel. They later found out that they had to work for their small rations of fuel and anything else they required, or were able to purchase. There was a small oven, but no food in the hut, and they had almost finished the rations they had brought with them.

Thus began the most uncomfortable, coldest, and hungriest time of their lives. There was no perimeter fence or guards. They were not needed as there was nowhere to run.

The following morning, they paraded in the cold as they were ordered. Many of the men, including Jakub and Filip, were marched out into the local forest area where they received instructions in the cutting down and branch stripping of trees for transportation to various parts of Russia, to be used as house building material and fuel.

They had arrived at the camp at the start of the winter. The temperature at this time was about -20 degrees, but over the next few months, it would sometimes drop as low as minus 40 to minus 60 degrees, making it impossible to carry on with this task. The men were required to work throughout the daylight hours, wearing only the clothing they had taken with them and a meagre quantity of food.

Adriana and Alicja became part of the camp kitchen staff, baking black bread and making watery rice soup, the only food the camp would provide. They were watched constantly by the guards, and any unauthorised morsel of food they took for themselves was subject to severe punishment. The work was twelve hours a day with one day off on Sunday.

In January, as it became colder, Jakub, Filip and dozens of other men were taken off forestry work and ordered onto unheated trucks at 7am each morning to be driven ten miles to the Malachite or Copper mines, where they were lowered two kilometres into the earth, forced to walk another two kilometres to the work face, then spend at least ten hours hacking at the rock face, while local Russian skilled mine workers shored up the overhanging rocks as they worked. The prisoners were weak through lack of nourishment and there were many serious and fatal accidents, and often, fewer men returned to the camp in the evening than had left that morning, to be casually replaced the next day by newcomers. The dead were simply placed in small side tunnels and sealed in.

With the cold weather, lack of food and strenuous work, sickness, including typhoid and cholera, became rife in the camp, and there were a large number of deaths. The prisoners themselves had to deal with the dead. The stronger prisoners had to dig graves. The ground was frozen, and it sometimes took several days to dig two metres into the ground, the diggers being forced to build fires to soften the earth in advance.

The miners were paid a small amount of money which they were allowed to spend in a local shop. That is when the shop had anything that they could buy, which was always a meagre amount.

As spring arrived, the family were suffering like most in the camp. They were thinner and weaker by far than when they arrived.

One of the Russian guards, Alex, had seemed to be a little more approachable than the rest, so Jakub spoke to him and told him that he and his son were skilled dairymen, if there was any employment on a local farm. The guard was reasonably sympathetic, and told Jakub that there were no farms as such. Many Siberian families, in a similar manner to many Polish families, kept for their own survival, two, three, and four cows and heifers. He was a local man, and would make it know in the area that there were prisoners of some skill in case of problems. That was all he could do.

Alex came back to Jakub early one April morning as he was getting ready for work. It was about a week later. He had spoken to an old school friend, a local landowner, who had a large house and grounds several miles from the Gulag. The man was Ivan Ivashov. He had ten cows, some heifers, and a bull. He was a businessman and did not regard himself as a farmer. He had a local man and woman seeing to the animals for him. One of his workers had been taken quite seriously ill with typhus, and he was looking for temporary replacements.

'He has a small building on his land which you and your family could use. I have spoken to the Camp Commandant, and he has said that I can take you there and leave you until he no longer has any use for you. We can go now. Please get your family ready. Take with you whatever possession you have. You may not be given the same hut on return.'

Mixed feelings of nervous apprehension and utter delight fell upon the family getting away from the Gulag, even for a short time.

The journey to the house took half an hour, and they could see the lovely spring Siberian countryside for the first time without a deep covering of snow. The few houses they passed, sat in one or two acres of land with the beginnings of vegetable patches fenced off from two or three cows.

On arrival at their destination, Alex pulled up outside a large, stone-built house, sat in many acres of land. The family alighted as the guard knocked on the door. Ivan Ivashov, a large, heavily bearded middle-aged man, came through the door. He shook hands with Alex then he saw in front of him four, filthy, ragged, lice-ridden, thin people.

'My God! What do they do to you at that accursed Gulag? Follow me.'

Alex drove away quickly before Ivan was able to turn and chastise him, feeling slightly ashamed of the condition of the prisoners he was partially responsible for.

Ivan walked them to the rear of the house and ushered them into a small, stone-built annex.

'This was a stable, but we don't keep so many horses anymore. You can light a fire when you need one. There are beds, fresh water, and a toilet outside. I will have someone bring you food. I can do nothing about your clothes for now, but you can now wash and darn them.'

The family were, by now, well advanced in the Russian language. They understood and were relieved by what was said. The sound of cattle in distress could clearly be heard and Jakub dared to speak up.

'Do your animals need immediate attention?'

'Yes. I was coming to that. We have been struggling to look after them.'

He took the family to the nearby barn, and they could see cows desperately in need of milking.

'We must do this before anything else,' said Jakub.

They could see all the equipment they needed and the whole family set about the task with Ivan looking on with pleasure. He could immediately see that he had taken on the right people for the job in hand, and vowed to himself that he would look after them the best he could during their stay with him.

# Chapter Seven

The time came for Boris to leave the dairy farm where he had been made most welcome. Jan had treated him more like a lost son than a worker. He could now speak and understand enough, he hoped, of the German language, together with the identity cards of the German ally Olek Adamovich, to see him safely to France. He had, by now, grown a thick beard and even Jan thought that he looked enough like the photograph to get by.

On the advice of Jan, he had waited a few days longer than he had intended for the day when Gust, who knew the area well, would be on a regular run taking beef, cheese, and butter across the German border to Dresden. He knew the area well.

In the early morning of Monday 14th January 1940, on the advice of Jan and Gust, they wound a bandage around Boris's left leg and applied a little bull's blood, which seeped slightly through his trousers for effect. His left arm was also bandaged and set into a sling. Jan had shaped a tree branch into a crutch to give the appearance of a wounded soldier. He was given Reichsmarks and a pack of food and drink, and he was ready to go.

After an almost tearful goodbye from Jan, Gust and Boris set off for the German border. Boris refused to hide in the truck as a safeguard for Gust. If he was arrested at the border, he instructed Gust to say that he had hitched a lift and that his passenger was unknown to him. They sat together in the front seats. It was a long drive and they chatted, as well as Boris was able, in German.

At the border, it was clear that Germany, by now, had full control of western Poland and regarded it as part of Germany. There were border guards, but they were simply waived through without any checks.

During the long drive to Dresden, traffic was light, and they were able to make good time. They arrived outside the main railway station in Dresden two hours later, and Gust, who had also grown fond of Boris, wished him the best of luck on his journey. He approached the station entrance and saw that there were two uniformed officers checking the identity of people queueing to enter.

'My first test,' he mused anxiously. 'I have to do it.'

Using his crutch, he limped forward and joined the long queue.

When his turn eventually came the guard said to him brusquely in German.

'Identity papers.'

The guard looked at the cards suspiciously and said, 'You're a Soviet soldier.'

Boris replied in his rough German.

'Yes, a friend of Germany. I was wounded in eastern Poland, and I am travelling to Koblenz to my sister who is married to a German businessman.'

'Why are you travelling there?'

'She is a nurse and will look after and heal me.'

'What is your name?'

'Olek Adamovich.'

The guard was still clearly suspicious and took the cards into the office behind him. He emerged after a few minutes gave the cards back to Boris and simply nodded his head, at which a very relieved Boris walked into the station. Gust, who was watching quietly from across the road, was very pleased that he could report back to Jan a positive start.

Boris bought his ticket. It was now late afternoon and the next train to Koblenz, where the Rhine and the Mosel rivers meet in the west of Germany, was not until 10 o'clock the following morning. He found himself a spot in a corner of a busy café and waiting area, to sit out the long hours before the train was due.

As time went on, the area became quieter with just a few people waiting for morning trains. Boris fell asleep in his corner. He was not disturbed during the long night and the following morning, when with some difficulty because of his bandaging, he was able to use the station toilet and wash before the train arrived.

Just before 10am, he boarded the train and found a window seat in a compartment. The train began to fill and to his horror many of his fellow passengers were German soldiers, two of whom entered his compartment.

They chatted together until after about half an hour and to his dismay one of them addressed him saying, 'Are you a wounded soldier?'

He replied, pretending to struggle even more with his broken German.

'Yes. I was wounded fighting the Poles on the eastern front.'

'Ah, you're Russian.'

'Yes, Olek.'

'We are Kurt and Hans.'

Boris relaxed, and they chatted on and off in an easy manner for the next hour, until most of the German soldiers left the train at Leipzig.

After they had gone, Boris was left wondering what this dreadful war was all about. The people he had been talking to were just ordinary, pleasant young men. He quietly concluded that war was not about the wishes and desires of ordinary people but was more about the ego and machinations of the so called powerful.

Some hours later, they stopped at Fuda, when a woman with two children entered his compartment. They spoke to other passengers in German, but when they became alone with him in the carriage, they began to speak, to Boris's consternation, in Ukrainian. He pretended to sleep until one of the playing children tumbled into him.

'I'm so sorry,' the woman said in German.

'It's okay, please don't worry,' he replied in the same language.

'You're not German.'

'No.'

He then foolishly attempted to imitate the Ukrainian manner of speaking.

'I am Ukrainian like you.'

She smiled and said, 'No – you are Polish.'

His heart sank. Had it been so easy to find him out? Was she about to report him to the soldiers still aboard the train?

'Are you a Polish soldier escaping from Poland?'

'I am not a soldier. My family were farmers, killed by German bombing. I am trying to escape to France where I have relatives,' he lied.

'Don't worry. We won't give you away. We live in a town near Koblenz where my husband is a German business man. Most of our townsfolk are against the war. We don't understand why the Fuhrer wants to dominate Europe when we live in this beautiful country.'

He again relaxed in the wonderful company of Olga Krugger and her children during the hours travelling to Koblenz. During their conversations, Olga recommended that Boris take a train from Koblenz to Luxemburg, then travel on to France. She also advised him not to leave the railway station and offered to book the ticket for him.

He refused saying, 'If I am arrested, I don't want you to be involved.'

They arrived in Koblenz at 5.30 in the late afternoon, and Boris wished Olga and her family a safe journey home. He immediately went to the ticket office and without any difficulty, purchased a ticket to Luxemburg city. He was pleased to hear that the train left one hour later and was only a three-hour journey. After a short wait, he boarded the train and again sat quietly by a window, hoping not to speak to anyone until they reached Luxemburg.

The train was stopped at the border and several guards entered and began checking the identity papers of everyone aboard. Boris was again, afraid of arrest. What he did not know was that the guards had a particular quarry in mind. His turn came and he produced his cards, anxiously trying not to show fear. The guard glanced at his papers, then handed them back, not showing the slightest interest. From the next carriage, he heard a shout 'Juden' and screaming and crying taking place. He did not understand until a fellow passenger said in German, 'They are searching for Jews.'

He heard passengers being taken from the train with much shouting and crying. The guards left and the train passed over the boundary into Luxemburg. Boris felt great relief for himself, but he also had a feeling of deep sorrow for the people taken from the train.

At Luxemburg city railway station, he changed his Reichsmarks to Francs and decided that a night in a hotel would refresh him for the remainder of his journey and he could perhaps find out where, if anywhere, the Polish army were located in France. He found a relatively cheap boarding house where he enjoyed an evening and night of freedom. He especially enjoyed the opportunity to rid himself of the bandages.

The following morning, after a good sleep and before returning to the railway station, he found a shop selling second hand clothing. He bought a pair of trousers and got rid of his bull's blood-stained ones. He then returned to the station, and still unaware of the location of a Polish army in France, indeed, even if one existed, he bought a ticket for Paris. He boarded at 11 in the morning. The three-hour journey was very pleasant with an excellent lunch and a glass of wine thrown in. He was now relaxed enough to enjoy the beautiful countryside. He alighted at Paris East Station and was at a complete loss. He spoke no French. He asked a few passers bye if they spoke German, to receive nothing but glaring looks and shudders from them. He changed to Polish with no better results.

Boris left the station and began to ask people in the streets the same question using both languages. Eventually, after an hour had passed, he got a result. A middle-aged woman said, 'I am Polish. How can I help?'

He explained his situation and his wish to join up with a Polish army in France, if such a thing existed.

'What is your name?'

'Boris Batrosz.'

'My name is Maria Nowak. Come with me Boris. I live nearby on the Rue de Messageries close to several Polish families. You will get all the information you need from them.'

It was now 4 in the afternoon, and Boris happily followed Maria to her home where he met her husband Alexsy. He made Boris feel at home and offered him a bed for as long as he wanted.

Alexsy had only one arm. He explained to Boris that he lost his left arm during the closing stages of world war one. If he was younger and fit, he would happily join Boris and join the Polish army which he was aware were forming somewhere to the west of France.

'How can I find out where?' said Boris.

'Young Adam Budny. He's about your age and he has been talking about joining the army during the last few days. I will go for him. He will know where.'

Thus, Boris and Adam met and were to become lifelong friends.

'After hearing Boris's traumatic story, Adam said, 'How long is it since you relaxed over a couple of beers?'

'Can't remember – never I think.'

'Okay, my treat. Let us go. Are you coming Alexsy?'

'No. You boys enjoy yourselves.'

In the bar, Adam told Boris that he intended to leave Paris a couple of days from now to travel to Parthenay on the west side of France, hoping to join the Polish army being formed there by General Wladyslaw Sikorski, the leader of the Polish Government in exile, and would be delighted if Boris could join him on the journey. The pair enjoyed each other's company greatly. Two days later, the intrepid pair, who were now firm friends, set off on the seven-hour train journey to find and to join the Polish army.

# Chapter Eight

The Gorka family were settling in beautifully in the old stable block. It was warm and comfortable. Food, and to some extent, clothing was provided by Ivan, and after a few days, they were looking more like their old selves.

The work was comparatively easy with just ten cows, four heifers and one bull to look after. It was early summertime and the animals were able to go out to pasture each day. Milking morning and late afternoon and keeping the barn clean was something that they had been well used to.

Filip was given the task of taking milk out in a churn to some of the local poorer families. Ivan had told him that the people were his tenants, and occasionally, when the need arose, did jobs and repair work for him around his estate. Because of that, he made no charge for the milk he provided. Filip was therefore surprised when he was offered payment by the families he supplied. He refused the payments to their delight. Just one woman glowered at him, and snatched her jug from him when he filled it. He thought no more about it, not even mentioning it, at first, to his own family.

Some weeks later and to their joint surprise, they found butter and cheese making equipment hidden away in a corner of the hay loft. It was filthy and had clearly been lying there for years. This equipment was pointed out to Ivan who, when he was not away on business, was a regular visitor to the stable and barn.

'What can you do with it?' he asked.

Jakub replied, 'We need to strip it down, clean and oil it, maybe make some new parts for it, and we can make butter and cheese for you and your tenants if you like.'

'I remember when I was a child, we always had fresh butter and cheese in the house. I was taken away by my mother to live in Moscow and only came back here ten years ago after my father died to take over the place. Butter and cheese never entered my head until now. Yes, by all means let us have butter and cheese once more,' he said laughing, throwing back his head and raising his arms in pleasure.

That night, before they retired, the family discussed the find. They decided that it appeared that the equipment had been hidden away deliberately. They all knew that cheese making, in particular, was a hard-working, arm-aching and a long process, not something for the weak-bodied or minded. It was then that Filip spoke about the tenants having to previously pay for their milk and the woman who did not seem pleased. They all commented on the dire state of the animals barn and equipment when they arrived. A decision was made not to speak about it again. They did not want to rock their presently fine and well-balanced boat.

Thus, the family spent the happiest summer since their incarceration doing what they knew best. They were now fit, healthy, and clean, with clothing bought by money paid to them by Ivan. New calves were born, some were distributed among the tenants of the estate, and others were kept and nurtured for the future. Milk, cheese, and butter was produced, and Ivan their benefactor was a very happy man.

It was the end of September. Summer was coming to a close and autumn beginning to set in, when a new man and woman appeared on the scene. They were brought to meet them by Ivan. He introduced them as Vadim and Kira Volkov. Filip recognised Kira as the woman who did not seem happy with free milk. Then, as Ivan spoke, he realised why she was unhappy with that situation. Ivan explained that they were the people who looked after his cattle before them and that Vadim had been very ill with typhus. He had been well looked after by Kira, and now he had recovered, they were looking to resume their work. Collectively, the family's hearts began to sink. Were they being sent back to the Gulag?

Then Ivan said to Jakub, 'You have much extended your duties since you have been here, with the extra cattle, and cheese and butter making, that I though two extra hands would be useful, but you Jakub are in charge'.

Their collective hearts lifted at the news, but the faces of Vadim and Kira told the opposite story.

Later that evening, before they retired for the night, Filip quietly told his family that he believed that Vadim and Kira had been selling the milk when they were in charge and pocketing the money. He had heard whispers on his milk round that they paid for their milk before he came. Again, in the hope of harmony, they decided to say nothing.

The pair who obviously needed the money, did the work Jakub allocated for them with a degree of reluctance. Vadim said that he would prefer to return to the milk round, but Jakub would not allow that, much to Vadim's displeasure.

Neither of the pair were happy with the arm-wrenching duties of cheese and butter making which Vadim performed so lazily and grumpily, complaining that his illness had debilitated him. The mixture was often spoiled, so Jakub reluctantly found him less strenuous duties.

Ivan called to see Jakub.

'I will be away on business in Moscow for a couple of months. Please carry on the way you are, and I will see you all on my return.'

Having heard the news, Vadim and Kira conspired that evening at home.

The following day, Kira turned up alone for duty saying that Vadim was not well. Vadim, who was perfectly well, attended the Gulag and asked to speak to a senior officer about a serious breach of the Gulag rules. He was shown into the Commandant's office.

'Well – what can I do for you?'

'The Gorca family who are supposed to be working on the Ivashov estate. They were taken there whilst I was ill. Now I am back. Ivan Ivashov is away, and they are malingering there, selling his milk, cheese, and butter for their own profit, otherwise doing nothing while I do all the work.'

'Okay. You will return to the estate with my men, point them out and we will return them to do some proper work.'

'Please do not inform Mister Ivashov. I would not want him to get into any trouble or to blame himself for their idleness. I will tell him that their time was up, and they have been returned.'

The family were as busy as ever on the estate, milking and doing all the other chores required, when a lorry rolled up. Five guards and Volkov alighted.

'Those four there,' he shouted.

Without any questions, explanations, or time to pack their belongings or food, the four were ushered into the rear of the lorry and taken immediately back to the Gulag. The Volkov's were left with big smiles on their faces. 'Happy times are here again,' they sang.

The family were pushed into a wooden hut, just as filthy as the one they were issued with initially and told that their future duties would be allocated the next morning. To say that they were devastated would be an understatement. It was now early October and the winter they feared was imminent.

The next morning in the Commandant's office, they were informed that in the future, they would be regarded as criminals for taking advantage of their master whilst he was away. All four were condemned to the Malachite mines. They would be taken to the mines each morning, Monday to Saturday, and returned after each twelve-hour shift. They would carry out the duties allocated to them by the mines' foremen. Jakub attempted to speak in their defence. The moment he opened his mouth, he was cracked hard on the back of his head by a guard and told to shut up. They had obviously been tried, convicted, and sentenced.

Thus began the most gruelling winter of their lives, with Jakub and Filip working the face of the mines with picks and shovels, and Adriana and Alicja pushing fully loaded trolleys from the mine face to the loading area and returning the empty ones for refilling. The only sustenance to keep them going being black bread and thin rice soup, until they became friendly with some of the local regular mine workers who felt for them and began to quietly slip them more nourishing food.

Their only blessing during this period was that whilst they were down the mine, they were away from the body-numbing Siberian temperatures.

The winter was interminable, the worst they had ever endured. But inevitably, the spring arrived at last, and it seemed to them that either they had served their sentence, or their crimes were forgotten. The men were re-allocated duties in the forest, cutting down and pruning fallen trees, and the ladies returned to kitchen duties. Life became marginally more tolerable.

On the 22nd June 1941, Germany began the invasion of the Soviet Union, and a pact was agreed between the London based Polish Government in exile and the Soviet Union to release Polish prisoners.

The Gorca family were one of the few families who had survived their incarceration intact, and together with many others, the Polish prisoners were suddenly released without explanation, food or financial support from the Gulag.

As they were preparing to leave, Ivan walked into their hut. He was immediately appalled by their sorry condition.

'I knew that you were about to be released, so have been to see the Commandant. He has told me what Vadim Volkov said to get you all reincarcerated. Will you please come back with me to my estate where I can get you cleaned up and fed before you decide what you will do in the future?'

The family happily obliged.

Back at the estate, Ivan invited them into the stable where they had lived. They found it in a vile and filthy state, the butter and cheese making equipment stacked in a corner, unused and dirty. He sent a messenger to find Vadim and Kira and to send them to him. He explained that he had been told by Vadim that the family had been recalled as a matter of course by the Commandant. He had since found that Vadim had been lying and had in fact engineered their return. As he spoke, the smiling couple walked into the old stable. As they saw the family sitting in a corner, their smiles rapidly faded, particularly when they saw the stern look on the face of Ivan Ivashov.

'I have just four things to say to you. One, I am now aware from my tenants that you are selling my milk to them for your own profit. Two, you lied to the Gulag Commandant and later to me about this honest family. Three, you are both fired. Four, you are my tenants and if you cause me or this family any more trouble you will be ejected from your home. Please leave now and never return.'

They left with despondent looks on their faces and slumped shoulders. Ivan then said to the family, 'Please come with me.' He led them to the rear door of the mansion and invited them into the kitchen, where they were given a sumptuous meal and later, to a suite of comfortable rooms on the ground floor, with windows overlooking the expansive moorland where the cattle were pastured. There was a small kitchen, a lounge and two bedrooms.

'Please, become my paid servants and this suite is yours for the rest of your lives.'

The family were, at first, too shocked to speak. Filip was the first to recover.

'That is an incredible offer. But I have heard that General Wladyslaw Anders has been released from a Soviet prison and is beginning to form a Polish army at Buzuluk in the south of the Soviet Union. It is my intention to travel there and join that army.'

Alicja then said, 'I am going to travel with Filip and hope to join that same army as a nurse.'

At that stage, Jakub and Adriana suddenly realised that the family was going to be split up for the first time, and they felt saddened and tearful by that thought.

'What about you?' said Ivan, looking at them.

'We have to say a very grateful 'yes' with many thanks,' said Adriana, with Jakub solemnly nodding.

Filip and Alicja agreed to stay with their parents until the milk and cheese making process was back in good order and they were back to their previous level of fitness, then they would leave.

It was towards the end of July when at last, Alicja and Filip bade a tearful farewell to their parents, and with money and food in their possession, they set off on a new and long journey to join the Polish army.

# Chapter Nine

It was mid-February 1940, when Adam and Boris travelled west by railway, a four-hour journey through beautiful French countryside to reach Parthenay some four hours later. When they arrived at the still forming vast Polish army camp, they joined a short queue of others, some in civilian clothing as they were, and others in care worn uniform, waiting to speak to officers in a reception area. They eventually reached the desk of a senior Sergeant. Adam had heard rumours that they may be sent away if they had no previous army experience.

The Sergeant said, 'You're together?'

'Yes,' said Adam. 'We would like to join the same unit.'

'Previous army experience?'

Adam had been practicing the answer to this question and said, 'Fourteenth Greater Polish Infantry at Poznam'.

The Sergeant looked at the young faces of both men, smiled and said, 'We won't send you to that unit in case the Commander does not recognise you and thinks that you may be soldiers of some experience.'

He requested their names, dates of birth, and the name and address of next of kin. Boris was unable to give the latter explaining, 'My parents were both killed by a German bomb.'

The Sergeant nodded with some sympathy.

'Okay, go into the far-right hand corner of this room where you be medically examined. If you are fit, you will both be taken to be handed uniforms, then you will go to join one of our two Independent Brigades and *begin…*' he said emphasising the word, 'your army training. Good luck to you both.'

They were both found to be fighting fit and with their new uniforms, they were escorted a kilometre into the camp where they found wooden huts, the home of the Independent Brigade.

Inside a hut they were met by a second Sergeant who told them to strip out of their civilian clothing and don their uniforms.

'What experience have you got?' the Sergeant demanded.

This time they were truthful and admitted, 'None.'

'Okay. It's getting late now. I will take you to your beds. Tomorrow morning you will hear the reveille and I want you on parade, smart, beds made within five minutes, understood?'

'Yes Sergeant.'

He took them into a barrack hut where they saw about forty other young men sitting on their beds and chatting. The Sergeant shouted, 'Lights out in one hour,' and left the hut.

Within that hour, Adam and Boris got to know several of their fellow privates, some who were new to the army like themselves.

At the sound of reveille the following morning, the whole hut was suddenly in turmoil, men dressing, bed-making, and rushing to get outside for the allotted time.

During their first few weeks, the pair were taught what it means to be a Polish soldier, drill and discipline, survival and field craft, first aid, and health and fitness. It was explained to them that they would have been taught weapon use, but the inefficient French Authorities had not yet provided weapons, even though they were assembling with the intention of defending France from a German attack.

At the beginning of March 1940, antiquated rifles and other weapons began to arrive, and the Independent Brigade began to train in their use. It was common knowledge by this time that the German army was beginning to mass behind the French defensive Maginot Line which extended along the borders of Italy, Switzerland, Germany, Luxembourg, and Belgium.

By the end of April, it was obvious that the attack would come soon. Adam and Boris's unit had now had brief training with the old weapons and were dispatched to defend the northern city of Reims. Other still unarmed members of the Polish army were sent to local ports to travel to Britain to begin to form a Polish defence presence there.

On the 10th May, the German army began their blitzkrieg, completely bypassing the Maginot line and attacking through the low countries of Luxembourg and Belgium. The attack was so fierce that nothing available at that time could stand in its way. The Polish army lost many men during that mighty struggle and along with British and French units were eventually forced to slowly retreat towards the northern French coast.

By the 22nd May, the Polish forces had reached an area just a few kilometres from Dunkirk where they knew that the evacuation of allied troops was taking place. They turned to defend that area, and, on that day, a fierce battle took place between the Polish infantry, British, and other allied units and their German enemies. The allies managed to hold their ground.

The next day, they expected to suffer a heavy defeat. Something strange happened. Much to their relief, the German army made no attempt to move forward that and the following day. They appeared to be resting.

Late on the 25th May, the remnants of the Polish army were ordered to move to the beaches and allow themselves to be evacuated to England. Adam and Boris were, by now, in poor shape but still alive.

The following day, the unit waded out into the sea at Dunkirk to be picked up by small vessels and transferred to a warship in the harbour. The ship was the destroyer HMS Shikari, the last warship to leave Dunkirk during the evacuation. Adam and Boris found themselves to be amongst 380 other allied soldiers aboard. The ship was heavily attacked by German war planes and even though she was lightly gunned, she made it home to Ramsgate with the surviving troops.

On arrival in Ramsgate, the Polish troops were gathered together by their officers, and after a rest and refreshments were transferred by train to the outskirts of Glasgow in Scotland where the Polish 1st Army Corps was being founded. They would remain there in full training until called for.

# Chapter Ten

In July 1940, 145 Polish pilots, including Albin, joined the Royal Air Force. At first, the British were sceptical of the abilities of these pilots who had now to be trained in the use of new and more modern types of aircraft, and had to be taught everything from scratch. The scepticism arose from the speed of which they were defeated by the German Air Force over Poland and France. The British were failing to take into account the numbers and age of the Polish aircraft compared with that of their enemy. It soon, however, became clear to the British that the Polish pilots were extremely skilled, experienced, and eager to fight, and they soon became an integral part of the Royal Air Force.

In August that year, the Luftwaffe launched an all-out assault against Britain, seeking to destroy the Royal Air Force before a full land invasion. The heroism and determination of the Allied Air Forces fighting many battles until the end of October that year, resulted in the winning of the Battle of Britain, which proved decisive in the eventual outcome of the war itself.

The Polish nurse Olga Andrysiak, who was now being forced to follow the German army, treating their wounded as they moved north towards Moscow, she heard on the grapevine that General Anders was forming a Polish army in Buzuluk in the southern part of the Soviet Union. She was a highly skilled and dedicated nurse and even though she was treating the enemy, she did so with kindness and compassion, but always longing to be back among her own people. She waited for the right moment when the field hospital was again uprooting to keep up with the army, and all personnel were occupied with the move. Then very early one morning, as they began the journey north, she escaped along a path into a deeply wooded area and began the long journey south on foot. Wearing just her nurse's uniform, overcoat, and shoes, she walked all the rest of that day fearing pursuit. She feared spending long nights in the cold open countryside. Fortunately, as evening came, she came across a dairy farm and could hear cattle lowing inside a barn.

'Ha! A good place to sleep,' she thought.

The door was unlocked and above the cattle she could just see a hay loft in the twilight. Climbing in, she settled down and slept.

She woke with a startled jerk early the next morning, to find a man staring down at her. At first, she thought she had been discovered and would either be shot for desertion or returned to the field hospital. Her fear was dispelled when she heard the man speak.

'You're a nurse.' he said in Russian, which she could partially understand. 'Have you been sent to see to my lad?'

Greatly relieved she said, 'No. Why, is he ill?'

'He fell off the farmhouse roof yesterday and broke his leg. He's in agony and I have sent for assistance.'

'Take me to him'.'

She found the young boy lying in bed with a broken shin bone in his left leg which was untreated.

'Have you any bandages and flat pieces of wood which I can make splints out of.'

The farmer went off and came back with suitable equipment.

'What's your name?' she said.

'Reuben.' he gasped, obviously in great pain.

'Reuben, this is going to hurt while I reset your bone, then you will start to feel better.'

To the farmer and his wife, she said, 'Please hold his arms and his other leg and keep him as still as you can for a moment.'

Then using her great skill, she quickly pulled the leg and reset it bone to bone. The boy screamed in agony as she did so. The pain was such that he became unconscious and she was able to splinter and bandage his leg whilst he slept. The grateful farmer and his wife offered and provided Olga with a large breakfast.

As she finished her meal and pondered her next move, the Russian doctor Dima Glinski entered the farmhouse to be told that Reuben's leg had been set by the nurse. He examined the splints and bandaging and expressed his satisfaction. He spoke to Olga.

'What on earth is a Polish nurse doing wandering to so deep into Russian territory?'

She explained her situation to his sympathetic understanding. He was delighted that she had found the strength to abandon the German invaders and he offered to drive her the 50 kilometres to the railway station which would take her south towards her destination. He even gave her the rubles she would need for the journey and for food to sustain her.

Several hours later, she was aboard the train and settled in reasonable comfort for the long journey ahead through the Russian countryside, which after many hours stopped at Buzuluk.

On arrival she was directed to the large house, which happened to be the new budding Polish army HQ, where she was welcomed and met the second good medical colleague of the day, Polish doctor Aleksy Broz, who was delighted to meet a very experienced nurse.

'I am charged with setting up a medical centre in a house two doors down from here and you are my first new colleague.'

They went together to the house which they found to be huge and empty. They had only been here a short time when the army delivered beds, sheets, blankets, washing facilities, and indeed, well before they were ready, filthy, malnourished, and very sick patients began to arrive. Thus, began a very exhausting period of work for Aleksy and Olga, until over the next several days, another doctor and several nurses of varying experience began to arrive from the prisons and Gulags.

# Chapter Eleven

Filip and Alicja set off on their mammoth journey. They took the advice of Ivan to stay clear of the war-torn areas. First , they caught the Trans-Siberian railway to Moscow. They found the long journey much more comfortable than their previous encounter with Soviet railways. The staff were helpful and reasonably friendly. They had sleeping compartments, the toilets were chemical rather than a hole in the floor, and in August time it was rather warmer. There was food to be bought and the hours passed very quickly.

In Moscow, they had to pass a night in the station and were advised to buy food before catching a train for the very long journey to Buzuluk in the south. This was far less comfortable, with no food or sleeping accommodation available.

During that journey, the pair realised how lucky they had been to stay for so long at the manor, when they saw other Poles getting on the train at many of the stations along the way. Some were filthy, dressed in rags and lice ridden, others were thin and skeletal. They were simply lucky to be alive, and all travelling south to join what was becoming known as Anders army. General Wladyslaw Anders was the man in charge of forming the army with Soviet permission. He had recently been released from a Soviet prison and the initial intention was to form an army to fight the Germans alongside the Soviets.

At various points during the long and tedious journey, they could clearly see through the train windows masses of Soviet troops and armoured brigades preparing to meet the advancing German invaders. Alicja and Filip shared what food they had with as many of the unfortunates as possible.

Before their arrival at Buzuluk, all potential army recruits were advised by the train guard to leave the train at Koltubanka, some 30 kilometres away where enlisting was taking place. Alicja asked for his advice on joining the nursing staff. He was not certain, but said that he had heard that they were setting up a hospital unit at Buzuluk and she should travel there.

When Filip and all the other hopeful recruits left the train, Alicja stayed aboard and would not see her brother again for several weeks.

At Buzuluk station, Alicja was astonished by the clean and tidy nature of this small town, with large brick-built houses, and smart gardens. She saw a soldier obviously on sentry duty outside the gate of one of the larger houses and approached him.

'I am looking for the hospital, can you help me?'

'Yes, Madam. Two doors down that way,' he said, indicating off to his left.

He appeared to be friendly and her curiosity was aroused she asked.

'Whose house is this?'

'This is the new Headquarters of the Polish army.'

It was, by now, late in the afternoon when she knocked on the door of the large house he had indicated, and after a few minutes, a tall, slim lady in nurse's uniform answered.

'I am seeking to become a nurse in the Polish army,' said Alicja.

'Come inside.'

She was taken into an office just inside the front door.

'Please be seated.'

The lady who introduced herself as Head Nurse Olga Andrysiak said, 'What nursing experience do you have?'

'None, but I am a hard worker, and I am willing to learn.'

The nurse looked slightly disappointed by the answer but said, 'We have many patients and few nurses. If you will subject yourself to a trial for the rest of this day, then we will see.'

'Yes please.'

Alicja was taken to a small room where a man was seated on a bench. He was dressed in rags, filthy and so thin Alicja could see his ribs poking through, and flea bites where his shirt was torn. In a weak voice she heard him say, 'Please help me.'

The nurse said, 'This is a new arrival. He is malnourished, suffering from scurvy, lousy, and he stinks. He needs to be stripped and bathed before we can give him a hospital gown, admit him to a ward, and begin to feed him. All the equipment you need is in there,' she said, pointing to a small side room. 'I will return in one hour to see how you are coping.'

Some women would be appalled by such a task, but Alicja had been through hell in the Gulag and was made of sterner stuff. She entered the small room and found it to be a bathroom. She tested the taps and there was hot water to be had, which she poured into the bath. Alicja helped him to hobble painfully into the bathroom.

'Can you undress yourself or shall I do it?'

They undressed him between them. When naked, she could see that he had scabs all over his body.

'You poor man. You have been through even worse that my family.'

She assisted him into the bath where she bathed him, washing his hair and beard carefully. When he was out of the bath and towelled dry, she found a pair of scissors and trimmed his hair and beard, as she had done many times for her father and brother. Then using a special metal comb which she found, she rid him of as many nit eggs as she could and dressed him in a hospital gown.

'Thank you.' he said in a shallow voice.

When nurse Andrysiak re-entered the room, she found a grateful patient ready to enter the ward, nibbling on a small piece of bread given to him by Alicja. His old clothing and hair were bagged up and ready to be discarded. The bathroom was clean and tidy, ready for the next user.

'You have passed my test and I will enrol you as a trainee nurse and provide you with a uniform tomorrow morning when you have had a good night's rest. You look as though you need it. Come with me.'

As he alighted from the train at Koltubanka, Filip helped a man who was so ill and emaciated that he could hardly stand, let alone walk to the recruiting centre. Filip took him by the arm and assisted him to walk slowly to the centre where they stood in line with most of the other hopefuls who had left the train. An officer walked along the line of men and approached Filip and his bedraggled companion, pointing to him and shouting at two soldiers standing by, 'Hospital for this one.'

Filip was relieved of his burden. He was, in fact, considerably fitter that most of the potentials, and had no trouble passing the fitness tests. Thus, Filip Gorka entered Anders Polish army. At first, the army was suffering great difficulties. They had no uniforms to dress their troops, and food, which was supposed to arrive from Moscow, was sparse. Modern weapons were also scarce. Nevertheless, they began their training, marching and learning field crafts as best they were able, and after a few weeks, things began to improve, with 100,000 uniforms and modern weapons arriving from Britain, and substantial food coming in both from Britain and later from America, even though they had yet to enter the war.

Alicja was fast becoming a very able nurse at the local hospital. She was particularly delighted with the progress of Albert Bosko, the man she had bathed and fed upon her arrival. With good nursing, he had quickly recovered and now looked a little on the thin side, but otherwise hale and hearty. He was discharged from the hospital, and two soldiers arrived to take him to Koltubanka for enlistment. During the journey, he informed the soldiers that it was never his intention to join the army. He was trying the make his way from a coal mine in the south-east, where he had been held prisoner, to Brest in eastern Poland, from where he had been taken by the Soviets. He wanted to find his wife and family from whom he had been forcibly parted two years before. He was so malnourished and ill that he had made his way to the hospital at Buzuluk, and he now wished to carry on with his long journey.

One of the soldiers said, 'You will have to tell that to the recruiting sergeant at Koltubanka.'

He did so on arrival, to be met with, 'You have recovered in an army hospital. Lots of us have family that we miss and have not seen for years. Now you are fit you will join the army whether you like it or not.'

And he was enlisted.


Towards the end of 1941, the Anders army had reached almost 25,000 troops and civilians. People were still pouring in and the numbers were still growing wildly.

Early in December of that year whilst taking a role call, it was noted that Albert Bosko was missing from the ranks. A search was made and he could not be found. His Sergeant Aleski Adamik, told his Commander that he had heard that Bosko was constantly saying the he had been forced into the army, when all he wanted was to join his family.

'Brest is at least two thousand kilometres away. How would he get there?'

They decided that he would probably catch the Moscow train part way, then try to get another train to take him west, which Adamik said would take him to the battle front. They sent a message to the Soviet Authorities for the train to be searched at the next stop, and if Bosko was found, he was to be returned for Court Martial. Their theory was confirmed. Two hours later, Bosko was taken from a train two stations along the track and was immediately returned by Soviet soldiers to the camp.

The following morning, he was subject to a Court Martial. His only defence was that he never wanted to join the army and was trying to make his way to Brest, which was now part of the Soviet Union, to be re-united with his family. His defence was rejected, and he was condemned to death by firing squad which was to be carried out immediately. Outside, the squad were waiting. The outcome of the trial was obviously a foregone conclusion.

# Chapter Twelve

The Anglo and Soviet armies invaded Iran in September 1941, and space was made available for allied troops. It became particularly necessary for allied forces to secure and protect the oil wells which were so valuable to the war effort.

Anders army were becoming more professional by the day, and were more and more reliant upon Britain and the allies, particularly America after they joined the war in December 1941.

The army had one serious problem. During the period before the German invasion of the Soviet Union, the German and Soviet soldiers had executed great numbers of the more senior officers of the old Polish army. So-much-so, that their positions had now to be refilled by promotions. Many of the sergeants moved up a rank, creating vacancies. The more senior men of the lower ranks were promoted. Filip, who had been in the army but a short time, had so impressed those in command that to his surprise and delight, he became a Lance Corporal in charge of a small unit of men.

Stalin and the Soviet authorities were now providing food, arms, and equipment to a massive Soviet army, and the supplies to Anders army and civilian population began to dry up. The result was beginning to tell on the mass of people, the provisions for whom were now mainly coming from Britain, and the General requested a move away from the Soviet zone. Stalin eventually agreed and on the 18th March 1942, 74,000 Polish soldiers and 41,000 Polish civilians, including hundreds of sick and malnourished orphaned children from Soviet orphanages which had been poorly maintained, packed themselves and their equipment into their army trucks and moved to the port of Krasnovodski by the Caspian sea. There they were loaded onto ships and transported to Pahlevi in Iran. Olga, Alicja and other nurses did their utmost during the journey to administer medicines and food to the sick and ailing civilians, particularly the children. She also spent time seeking for her brother Filip among the thousands of Polish soldiers during the voyage, eventually finding him leaning against a rail looking out to sea. They were delighted to have found each other, promising that if they survived the war, they would never lose touch again.

Many died during the four-day journey, of malnourishment, cholera, typhoid, and other diseases caused by severe neglect. Many more died in the Iranian port of Pahlevi, where they were forced into quarantine by the Iranian Authorities, who in fairness, welcomed them and did their very best to feed the vast numbers. The areas of the quarantine were warehouses by the docks, where thousands were held including Anders army for many weeks.

In all, 3,000 Polish people died in Iran, mainly due to the forced conditions before their arrival.

Some weeks later, the army, including the nurses and auxiliary staff, travelled to Tehran, where for a time they were given the duties of guarding the many oil wells and the area of land overlooking the Persian Gulf. This became known as the Persian corridor, where ships sailed from the Arabian Sea via the narrow dog leg, into the Persian Gulf through which lend-lease food and armaments from the allies, and particularly America, flowed into the Soviet Union across Iran and through the Caspian Sea.

Because of great difficulties in supplying these things to the U.S.S.R. via the North Atlantic into northern Russia, due to the massive attrition by German submarines and the extreme weather conditions, the Persian corridor had become essential to the allied war effort.

After an interminable period in quarantine, the Polish army, now under British control, was sent to various parts of Iran to guards the oil wells essential to the war effort. Filip's group was allocated the Shiraz city area and the oil wells around that, where they practiced in the use of anti-aircraft weapons and other defensive tactics in case of German air-raids or para-troop invasion. They were there for many weeks, becoming proficient in the use of these defensive measures.

Weeks later, they were moved to the dogleg of the Persian corridor because of information that the Germans intended to commence an aerial bombardment of shipping, entering and leaving the Persian Gulf with lend-lease, oil supplies, and other essential goods. The bombardment never came.

Under British command, Anders brought his army back together. They had now acquired many trucks and other essential equipment, and under the orders of the British, they began the long journey from Iran, through the middle east and North Africa, travelling through Iraq and Syria to Palestine, where they rested awhile. In Palestine, some Jewish members of his army deserted. It would have been impossible to trace and arrest them all, particularly in a hostile environment, so they were left behind.

The army carried on through Jordan into Egypt and Libya to Tunisia, where they again rested. The Italian army had recently been defeated in Tunisia. It was now mid-June 1943, and the allies, under the command of Lieutenant General Patton and General Montgomery, were planning the Italian campaign, operation Husky. Italy and Tunisia were only a comparatively short distance from each other, 300 miles across the Mediterranean Sea.

Many of Anders soldiers had trained in the use of machine guns. It was decided to link two squadrons of the Polish army to the Independent Brigade training to take part in the Sicilian landings. Filip's unit was part of that force.

On the morning of the 9th July, he and thousands of others boarded ships in Tunis to assist the 8th army and airborne commandos, under the control of General Montgomery, and the American and Canadian armies under the command of General Patton, to fight and defeat the Axis, Italian, and German Fascist forces. The Allied army consisted of 150,000 troops, 3,000 ships, and 4,000 aircraft, facing an Axis army of 200,000 Italian troops, 32,000 German troops, and a Panzer division.

The following morning, the attack began landing on the beaches of southern Sicily, encountering fierce bombardment and defence, to the loss of many lives on either side.

As the forces cleared the beaches and began to move inland, the medical and auxiliary services moved onto the land and a large medical centre was created close to the shore. Doctors and nurses from all the invading countries were involved. Alicja and Olga were among those many nurses.

They had mainly been used to treating sick and malnourished people in the past, and it came as quite a shock, particularly for Alicja, to be treating men with bullet and shrapnel wounds, and legs and bodies ripped apart by mines and bombardment. Wounded men were arriving for treatment from all the nationalities involved in the war, including German and Italian soldiers.

The army slowly moved along the south-eastern coast, capturing the cities of Augusta and Catania before meeting strong joint German and Italian resistance at the Airforce complex of Gerbini.

Their next great obstacle was the rugged volcanic slopes of Mount Etna, where they became bogged down for several days due to strong Axis defence. Finally, breaking through this resistance, they could make their way to the port of Messina on the extreme east of the island where they met other British, American, and Canadian troops, who had, after many long and bitter battles taking place in the north and central parts of the island, had also made their way to the port. It had taken 38 days to capture the island and they were now just 40 miles from the Italian mainland.

At this time, Boris and Adam, whilst not actively engaging the enemy, were kept very busy in Scotland with the war effort. They were now part of the Polish 1st Corps, under General Sikorski. Their Headquarters was in the buildings and grounds of Barony Castle on the Scottish Borders at Peebles, where the staff office, training, and military schools were located. The soldiers were based in many districts of Scotland, where they were fully engaged with coastal defences, creating anti-tank barriers and pill boxes. They had taken responsibility for the manning and maintenance of armoured trains and many other war-time tasks.

Many of the troops had been under fire in Poland, the Soviet Union, and France, and were well aware that, come a German invasion of Britain, or a retaliatory attack by the allies, they would come under enemy fire once more, and they were ready and willing.

Many Axis forces had escaped from Sicily to the mainland at the conclusion of the battle and were ready to resist any future invasion. They considered this to be a victory.

On the 3rd September 1943, the early stages of operation Avalanche and Slapstick, the invasion of the Italian mainland, commenced. The Allied army attacked Italy on three fronts, troops coming from Oman, Tunis, and Tripoli. The attack at Calabria and Taranto, along the toe and arch of southern Italian foot, became bogged down by demolished bridges, mines, and road blocks. The slow movement became more of an engineering problem rather than a tactical one. It took time and patience, but the Allies eventually made progress towards other landings at Salermo.

Before the assault on Salermo on the 9th September, the Italian army agreed an armistice and stood down from the conflict. Indeed, some Italian forces were deeply unhappy with the German occupation of their country and were willing to assist the Allied effort where possible.

At Salermo, the Allies, at first, met with stiff resistance from the German army, which, after many bitter battles, pulled their troops back to the Gustav line which stretched all the way across the peninsula from the Mediterranean to the Adriatic.

As 1943 came to a close, the Italian campaign began to show signs of collapsing, such was the slow progress being made over the mountainous terrain where cold and hunger began to take its toll. Filip was among many Allied soldiers to suffer greatly during this period. It became apparent to the Allied leaders that if they were to progress, it was imperative to attack the old Benedictine Monastery of Monte Cassino perched on the top of a mountain, overlooking the town of Cassino and held by the German army. There were many tactical problems to overcome. To capture and break through at Cassino, the Allies had to cross marshy ground to reach the Rapido, a nine foot, deep, fast-flowing river.

There were four separate assaults on the Monastery, beginning when Allies troops crossed the river by night in boats. Even with the extensive use of aerial bombardment, that assault, and two following attempts to break through Cassino and head towards Rome, were repulsed by a strong German army, with the great advantage of height and numbers and the added incentive of stopping the Allies breaching the Gustav line.

Following many months of attempting to breach the line on the 16th May 1944, it became the turn of Anders Polish army to make the next attempt. It should be remembered that these were no ordinary conscripts, but mainly battle-hardened troops who had fought against the Soviets in Poland. On the evening before the assault, they were spoken to by their General who is reported as saying, 'Let the spirit of lions enter your hearts. Go and take revenge for all the suffering in our land, for what you have suffered for many years in Russia, and for years of separation from your families.'

The next morning, the Polish army attacked under cover of artillery fire from the Allies on the ground and aerial bombardment. Over that full day, they suffered many losses. The German army had no answer to the ferocity of the assault and in the end, they were driven from Monte Cassino and the Gustav line, at last, was breached. The Allies poured through to meet up with forces who had broken through the German defence further along the Mediterranean coast at Anzio.

1,072 Polish soldiers lost their lives at Monte Cassino, their graves in the beautifully kept cemetery are still there to be seen.

By June 1944, the Allied armies reached and held Rome. The German army retreated and the Allied Italian campaign was successfully completed.

# Chapter Thirteen

In February 1942, the Polish 1$^{st}$ Armoured Division (1 Dywizja Pancerna) was created in the Duns area in Scotland, Commanded by Major General Maczek. Bóris and Adam applied for, and were successful in joining this Division. At its height, the Division numbered 18,000 soldiers with 880 tanks of the Polish light 7TPs design, and many transport vehicles. Later, they were moved to the south of England to continue their rigorous training, together with Canadian tank units.

Just after midnight on June 6$^{th}$ 1944, 24,000 American, British, and Canadian airborne troops were flown into Normandy to commence Operation Overlord.

At 6.30 am that day, the Allied Infantry and Armoured Divisions began the D-Day landings along the Normandy coast. The beaches were given the operational names of Utah, Omaha, Gold, Juno, and Sword. After many fierce battles, in which many Allied and German soldiers were killed, over many months, progress was slowly made. The Canadian and Polish armoured forces fought their way to the Falaise area of France, and between the 12$^{th}$ and 21$^{st}$ August, they fought a battle against German forces, which proved pivotal to the success of Operation Overlord. 50,000 German troops were almost surrounded by the two armoured Divisions, when the Polish units found themselves on the top of a hill overlooking the German armies escape route. They closed the gap, completely trapping the Germans.

After Normandy, the Polish Division were sent to Belgium and the Netherlands, where, during fierce battles in the region of Breda, the Polish Division repelled all counter attacks and obtained the surrender of vast numbers of German soldiers. The vast impact the Polish Air Force and Army had in the conclusion of World War II and the Allied victory, cannot be overstated. Even the Navy took great honours when the ORP Piorun, an N-Class Destroyer on loan to the Polish Navy, located the giant German battleship Bismark, and drew its fire whilst other units of the Royal Navy caught and sank the ship.

The irony for those Polish people taking part in the war, is that they were forbidden, under pain of death, from returning to Poland, which was now under Soviet control. The reason for this was never known for certain. Some say that it was to prevent them from reclaiming their lands and property. Others say that they had begun to understand the concepts of freedom and democracy and would not take well to total control.

The displaced Poles settled around the world, in the United States, Canada, Australia, and Britain. 150,000 settled in the U.K. alone.

The importance played by Poles during the war was one factor. Another, was the need for workers in the early postwar years. Polish people were considered ideal immigrants, with many having experience in textiles, engineering, and agriculture, etc.

In the early part of 1946, Doctor Broz and his Polish army nurses were unable to return to Poland and were brought from Germany to Britain.

During the war years, they had become very experienced in all kinds of patient treatment, and during most of the previous two years, most of their patients had been American, British, Australian, or Canadian, and they had learned to speak the English language proficiently. It was the intention of the authorities to discharge them from army duties and to place them in various hospitals where possible, of their choice, throughout the country. Doctor Broz, who had been put in charge of the relocation of his nurses, called them into his new office to ascertain how he could help each individual.

Olga and Alicja were now the best of friends and they opted to see the doctor together.

'How can I help you ladies?'

Olga said, 'We are trying to locate three men. My husband Albin Andrysiak, and Alicja's brother, Filip Gorca, and her fiancée, Boris Bartosz, if indeed they are still alive.'

The good doctor took as many details of the three as he could, including their last known units, and positions, and their dates of birth. He had taken on similar tasks for some of his other nurses and colleagues, which had sometimes ended in great happiness, and other times in heartbreak and failure where friends and relatives had been killed or were seriously injured. He had been able to bring great joy into the lives of some, and devastation into the lives of others. He hoped for the best on this one. He also knew from previous experience, that the process would take a great deal of time, as so many people were searching for their loved ones.

In the past, he had spent many hours ringing the various Polish units, but on this occasion, he rang the War Office and was put through to a young woman, who was in fact doing exactly the same type of searches and collating the information he needed. She promised to search for the information he needed and get back to him.

Two days later, he was delighted when she rang to inform him that all three had survived the war and were now stationed in various parts of Britain. Sergeants Filip Gorca and Boris Batrosz were pending demobilisation, and Albin Andrysiak was now a Wing Commander and was staying on for a while at RAF Abingdon Oxfordshire.

'Is it possible for you to instruct all three to attend the Royal medical centre in Aldershot, without telling them exactly why, other than informing them that it will be greatly to their advantage?'

She agreed to do so, and arrangements were made for them to be at the centre at 12 noon in two days hence.

It was now early September 1946, when the three mystified men were greeted one at a time by Doctor Broz in the centres' reception area, and conducted to his secretary's office, where Filip and Boris recognised each other immediately and hugged.

Albin then said, 'Doctor, I hope that this is not bad news about our loved ones.'

The doctor smiled to alleviate his fears. He walked across the room and opened the door to his inner office, and the three ladies walked into the room. The good doctor stood for a moment enjoying the tears of joys and the emotion of the reunion before he walked away and left them to their obvious delight.

One month later, after all the trauma and anguish of World War II was behind them, Boris and Alicja experienced the happiest day in their still young lives, when they married at St Joseph's Romanesque Catholic Church in Aldershot, with Filip as best man and all their Polish army colleagues in uniform, packing the church and creating an arch with rifles as they left for a short honeymoon on the West Sussex coast. The only blight on the day was the fact that Boris's parents had died at the start of the war, and Alicja's parents were thousands of miles away in Siberia.

Both Filip and Alicja wrote to their parents informing them that they had survived the war, telling them of the wedding and asking for news of themselves. Olga was the first to leave the Polish army nursing corps having acquired a position at Oxford Military Hospital, in order that she could live with her husband at the nearby air base.

In early 1947, Filip and Boris were demobilised from the army and Alicja was free to leave the nursing corps. There were vacancies for nurses at Rossendale General Hospital in Lancashire, and plenty of farmland all around the town for the two men to find work. The intrepid trio set off for Rossendale travelling by train, and eventually alighting at Rawtenstall railway station. They were able to find temporary accommodation at the Queens Hotel in the town centre. When the local people realised that they had two ex-soldiers and a nurse in their midst, arriving in their town from the war and unable to return to their home because of ill will, the trio became very popular in the town, particularly among other returnees and people who had lost loved ones. They all now spoke excellent English and set about finding work.

Alicja had no problem in being taken on as a nurse. The two men, who were, at first, looking for jobs as farmworkers, were persuaded that they could earn more and spend more leisure time with their family if they took on work in the textile industry. They both applied for jobs in a local factory and were taken on as carders, a process which disentangles, cleans, and intermixes fibres, taking out dust and impurities. When Alicja was made aware of the work they had taken on she made them masks to keep the impurities from their lungs and insisted that they wear them whenever they were working.

Boris and Alicja applied for, and were granted, a council owned dwelling on Grange Road near the town centre. Filip was of course, their guest at the house, and insisting upon paying for his lodgings, an amount which covered one third of the council rent.

One of their great pleasures on each Saturday evening was to visit the Astoria Ballroom and dance to the band music of Glen Miller and others. On one of their visits in early 1948, Filip, who was now 28 years of age, caught the eye of Irene Waller, a tall, slim widow of similar age, who had lost her husband during the Normandy landings. She appeared to be alone. He asked her to dance a waltz, which he managed to do clumsily. At the end of which, he invited her to sit with his group at the table. To his surprise and delight she agreed to do so. That was the beginning of a wonderful relationship, which led to their marriage at St James the Less on Burnley Road, near her home, one year later.

Irene was the mother of a two year-old daughter and the owner of a small, stone-terraced house on Burnley Road. She was more than happy to share the house with Filip, and he in turn was delighted to be the stepfather of a lovely daughter Sarah.

Now, Boris and Alicja had a son, Joseph, and had moved on from their rented house to their own stone cottage nearby. The families were happy with their lot, especially when a letter came from Siberia from Jakub and Adriana saying that they were blessed with a third child, a son whom they had called Dariusz. Their joint delighted comment at the news was, 'Well, if they can have a child at their age, there is plenty of time for us'.

# Historical Note.
# World War 11 And Beyond

There are various estimations of the number of Polish citizens who perished during the conflict and the occupation of Poland by German and Soviet troops. It is generally estimated that the number was around 6,000,000.

At the end of the war, Polish people were not allowed to return to the places of their birth. Around 150,000 settled in the United Kingdom. Many others settled in the United States of America, Canada, and Australia.

In February 1945, the Yalta conference sanctioned a provisional government in Poland.

The Potsdam conference in July that same year, ratified the shift of the Polish frontier.

A communist-controlled Provisional Government was formed, completely ignoring the Polish Government in exile, which had been based in London since 1940.

In 1955, the Warsaw Pact, the collective defence treaty, was signed in Warsaw between the Soviet Union and several other Eastern Bloc Socialist Republics. Over a long period of time, many things began to happen (far more that I have listed here) which made a difference to the Polish people.

In 1978, Karol Jozef Wojtyla became 'Pope John Paul II' and he visited his native Poland in 1979.

In 1980, following a great deal of poverty and much political unrest, the union 'Solidarity' was formed under the leadership of Lech Walesa.

In 1990, Lech Walesa came to power in Poland. He was the first democratically elected President of Poland since 1926.

The Warsaw pact was dissolved in 1991 and the 'Social Democracy of the Republic of Poland' was formed. The last Soviet troops left Poland in September of 1993.

In 1999, Poland joined the North Atlantic Treaty Organisation.

This completed Poland's transition from Communist Party rule to a western style democratic political system. By this time, most of the displaced Polish people still alive were now in their seventies and eighties, settled in various parts of the world and very unlikely to return to re-settle.

## The End.